By Lee Kirby
Illustrated by George O'Connor

LITTLE SIMON
New York London Toronto Sydney New Delhi

If you purchased this book without a cover, you should be aware that this book is stolen property. It was reported as "unsold and destroyed" to the publisher, and neither the author nor the publisher has received any payment for this "stripped book."

This book is a work of fiction. Any references to historical events, real people, or real places are used fictitiously. Other names, characters, places, and events are products of the author's imagination, and any resemblance to actual events or places or persons, living or dead, is entirely coincidental.

LITTLE SIMON
An imprint of Simon & Schuster Children's Publishing Division • 1230 Avenue of the Americas, New York, New York 10020 • First Little Simon paperback edition December 2017. For information about special discounts for bulk purchases, please contact Simon & Schuster Special Sales at 1-866-506-1949 or business@simonandschuster.com. The Simon & Schuster Speakers Bureau can bring authors to your live event. For more information or to book an event contact the Simon & Schuster Speakers Bureau at 1-866-248-3049 or visit our website at www.simonspeakers.com. Designed by Jay Colvin. The text of this book was set in Little Simon Gazette.
Manufactured in the United States of America 0517 MTN 10 9 8 7 6 5 4 3 2 1
Cataloging-in-Publication Data for this title is available from the Library of Congress.
ISBN 978-1-4814-9997-2 (hc)
ISBN 978-1-4814-9996-5 (pbk)
ISBN 978-1-4814-9998-9 (eBook)

CONTENTS

1

ALL ALONE AGAIN

Can you keep a secret? Yes? Great. We'll come back to that. At the moment, that sure is one sad hamster who's moping in his cage. A hamster named Turbo.

Turbo hasn't eaten since yesterday. He doesn't even have the energy to jog on his hamster wheel.

And while he normally loves keeping a watchful eye on Classroom C—that's his duty as the official class pet—today he doesn't even feel like doing that.

Why, you might wonder?

Well, it all began with an evil rat named Whiskerface. Whiskerface's main goal in life was to try to take

over the world. Recently, he had tried to test out that plan right here at Sunnyview Elementary. But what he didn't expect was to have to face the Superpet Superhero League.

That brings us back to the big secret. You see, Turbo the hamster isn't your ordinary hamster. He's actually . . .

And he's a member of . . .

THE SUPERPET SUPERHERO LEAGUE!

The Superpet Superhero League is made up of all the class pets at Sunnview Elementary. Together, these superheroic pets have one mission: making sure the school is kept safe. And often this means battling evil like Whiskerface, flying ninja squirrels, and villains like the Pencil Pointer.

When Whiskerface tried to test out his world-takeover, the Superpet Superhero League had stood in his way!

But during the battle, Nell—also known as Fantastic Fish—had lost her home. She usually lived in a large aquarium in the hallway. That aquarium had shattered on the floor during the fight, so she'd spent the last week in *Turbo's* classroom, right next to his hamster cage! They had been having the best time.

Then, just yesterday, someone had come to take Nell away. It turned out they'd gotten her a brand-new state-of-the-art aquarium. Turbo knew he should be happy for Nell, but truthfully, he was sad to see her go.

Turbo was feeling pretty sorry for himself, when suddenly the school bell rang. His kids! He had lost track of time. It was the start of the school day, which meant all the students of Ms. Beasley's second-grade class would be entering the classroom soon. They always cheered him up. The kids loved

Turbo and often did drawings of him or brought him little treats. Today, one of his favorite students, a boy named Eugene McGillicudy, showed Turbo a drawing he'd done of himself as a superhero named Captain Awesome.

Turbo made little hamster noises of approval. After all, he couldn't actually tell Eugene how much he liked the drawing. That would give away

his supersecret!

The day went by surprisingly quickly despite the fact that Turbo didn't have his friend Nell next to him. Soon enough, the last school bell rang and the kids filed out of the classroom.

As soon as the school lights were off, Turbo climbed out of his cage and scampered down to the reading nook of Classroom C. That was where the Superpet Superhero League had their supersecret meetings, and it was time for today's!

GOOD SURPRISE OR EVIL SURPRISE?

Angelina, also known as Wonder Pig, was the first to arrive. The cover of the vent in Classroom C popped off and out she crawled.

That was how the Superpets got around the school—through the vent system! It was also how they communicated with one another. If there was ever trouble, a pet would tap something on the inside of the vent and the sound would echo throughout all the vents, alerting the rest of the pets to come quickly!

Angelina was followed by Leo, also known as the Great Gecko,

who came crawling out of the vent with Clever, also known as the Green Winger. Frank, also known as Boss Bunny, came next. He was with Nell!

Finally, slow as ever, came Warren. His superhero name was Professor Turtle.

With the Superpet Superhero League all there, the meeting could begin.

"First order of business," said Leo, who often ran the meetings. "Happy birthday, Angelina!"

Angelina blushed. "Thanks, Leo," she said.

Turbo didn't know it was Angelina's birthday! It wasn't that long ago that he'd even discovered there were other class pets, so he was still getting to know all of them.

"After we're done with our meeting, we'll all head to the cafeteria for a special treat," said Leo. "So, who has something to report?"

"Well, you guys have to come check out my new aquarium sometime," said Nell. "I now have five different types of coral. Five! And there's this awesome cave that I use as my top-secret headquarters."

All the superpets thought that sounded pretty cool.

"I perfected a new trick," said Clever. Being a bird, she was really acrobatic.

The rest of the pets clapped and cheered as Clever performed her impressive trick. When she landed, she bowed.

"I . . . have . . . some . . . news," began Warren.

The rest of the pets waited patiently for Warren to reveal the news. And when he did, they were more curious than ever. Warren told them that the science teacher, Dr. Garfield, had announced to his last class of the day that when they came back for science the next afternoon, there would be a surprise in the classroom.

As the pets headed to the cafeteria, they took turns guessing what the surprise might be.

"Nell's being moved back to my

classroom?" Turbo suggested hopefully. But even he knew that was a long shot.

"They're installing a roller coaster on the playground?" Nell offered.

"We get to eat human food all the time?!" Frank shouted.

"Not likely," said Leo. "But speaking of human food . . ." Leo trailed off as he gestured toward something that was on the floor in the middle of the cafeteria.

It was a half-eaten, slightly smushed cake with a candle in it.

"Isn't it beautiful?" said Leo proudly. "Frank and Clever helped me transport it from the teacher's lounge, and we even found a candle in the garbage!"

Angelina was beaming. "It's perfect," she told her friends. "Let's dig in!"

But Turbo was too distracted to eat at the moment. Warren had said there was going to be a surprise in the science lab. Sometimes surprises were good.

But sometimes . . .

they were evil.

3

IT'S A JUNGLE OUT THERE

The next morning, Turbo woke up especially early. He was still thinking about that surprise. And he hoped that whatever it was, Warren was okay.

Turbo thought about it all morning. While the kids in the classroom were taking a spelling test, he even considered trying to sneak out.

But he decided it was too risky. So Turbo waited for the day to end. He waited . . . and waited. And finally, the classroom emptied out.

I've got to go check on Warren, Turbo thought.

But before he could even move a muscle, the Superpet Superhero alarm sounded. Turbo knew right away it was Warren, even before he could tell that the object making the sound was a beaker.

Turbo threw on his cape and his goggles, and Super Turbo climbed out of his cage. He ran as fast as he could to the vents.

"Oof!" some-one cried as Turbo crashed right into them and bounced off. It was Won-der Pig. She was a lot bigger than

Super Turbo.

"Sorry, Wonder Pig," Super Turbo apologized. "I've just had a bad feeling about this 'surprise' all day."

"Me too," said Wonder Pig.

They continued down the vent and found the rest of the superpets along the way. As they all poured out into the science lab, they looked around for Professor Turtle.

"Oh no! We must be too late! Whatever the surprise was must have already taken our turtle friend!" cried Fantastic Fish, imagining the worst.

"Hey . . . guys . . . ," came a slow voice just then.

"Professor Turtle!" everyone cried. They were so happy to see him.

"So what's the big surprise?" asked Boss Bunny.

"I . . . don't know . . . yet. It's . . . up there . . . ," said Professor Turtle, gesturing to the science teacher's desk. The superpets all looked up.

"Well, as superpets, it's our duty to find out what exactly is up there," said the Green Winger. "I'll go take a look." She fluttered up to the desk.

"What is it?" asked Super Turbo from down below.

"I can't see anything!" cried the Green Winger. "It's like a jungle in here. Can someone else come up?"

When Super Turbo landed on the desk next to the Green Winger, he understood exactly what she was talking about. It really did look like a jungle in there! But what was living in that jungle? Surely, it was something terrifying!

Super Turbo pressed his face against the outside of the glass to get a better look. But at that very moment, something inside pressed its face up against the glass.

4
IT'S A BIRD, IT'S A PLANE,
IT'S A FIRE-BREATHING DRAGON!

Just as quickly as the face appeared, it disappeared. Super Turbo backed away.

"What. Was. That?" he asked.

The Green Winger shook her head. "I have no idea, but it was terrifying," she said. "Let's get the others up here." She called down to the rest of the team and they made their way up to the top of the desk.

THEY PULLED
BB

THEY ROLLED

Boss Bunny let out a whistle through his buck teeth. "Wow, whatever lives in there must be really wild," he remarked.

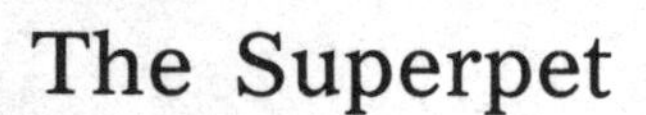

The Superpet Superhero League surrounded the terrarium. The Great Gecko suggested that if they really wanted to see this creature again, they should tap on the glass. He knew from experience that that was just about the most annoying thing anyone could do to a pet living in a terrarium.

"On the count of three," said Super Turbo. "One, two, three!"

They waited. And waited. And they were about to give up when suddenly the creature jumped out.

"AHHHHH!" all the superpets screamed. Fantastic Fish nearly rolled off the table in fear.

The creature was worse than Super Turbo could have imagined.

"Let's go!" Super Turbo yelled. And the superpets crawled, climbed, raced, and flew down from the desk.

Safely back on the ground, the animals all caught their breath. It took them a few minutes to calm down, but finally the Great Gecko spoke up.

"Does anyone know what that creature was?" he asked the team.

All of the animals shook their heads. All but one. Angelina was staring back up at the desk, as if in a daze.

"I do," she finally said.

The animals waited for her to continue.

5

AN UNLIKELY TEAM

After Angelina's announcement, the superpets raced back to the safety of Classroom C.

In the reading nook, they decided they needed to come up with a plan.

"The thing about fire-breathing dragons is—" began Angelina.

"That they can breathe fire?"

Clever finished Angelina's sentence.

Angelina nodded.

"So how do we get close to this creature without disturbing it?" Nell asked.

The superpets thought.

AND THOUGHT.

Frank snapped his fingers. "I've got it! Leo, since you look like a much tinier version of that dragon, maybe you can go and pretend to be a fire-breathing dragon yourself."

"And then what?" asked Leo. "How do we get the dragon out of the school without him or her doing any damage?"

Frank's excitement quickly faded. "I

haven't figured that part out yet."

"We could try to knock the dragon's terrarium off the table," suggested Angelina.

Turbo pointed out that they didn't want to *hurt* the dragon. But all this time

he had been thinking about something. He was almost afraid to tell the superpets his idea. It was risky. Very risky.

"Guys," Turbo began. "Whiskerface is always trying to get rid of us superpets, right?"

The other animals nodded.

"Well," continued Turbo, "even though his plans usually don't *work*,

that's because the Superpet Superhero League is there to stop him."

"Where . . . are . . . you . . . going . . . with . . . this?" asked Warren nervously.

"If we're not the ones stopping Whiskerface's evil plan, maybe that

plan would actually *work*. Maybe he could help us get rid of the fire-breathing dragon."

A few minutes passed and no one said a word. Turbo was starting to regret telling the animals his plan, when Angelina suddenly spoke up.

"You know what, Turbo?" she said. "This might be your craziest idea yet. But I think it might be genius. Who's with us?" Angelina went and stood next to Turbo.

Then Leo raised his hand and joined them.

He was followed by Clever, Frank, and Nell. Warren was the only one who still seemed unsure.

"This is my . . . home . . . we're . . . talking about," he said to them. "What if . . . Whiskerface . . . turns on us?"

"We'll be there to stop him," said Turbo. "We won't let anything happen to the science lab, Warren."

So, reluctantly, Warren joined the rest of the animals. Then the whole group made their way to the cafeteria.

The superpets knew that Whisker-face lived inside the pantry. Well, they knew he lived inside the *wall* of the pantry—so they headed straight there.

Boss Bunny's tummy rumbled. "Think we have time for a snack?" he asked.

"NO!" said the rest of the superpets at once.

Now to get the pantry door open.

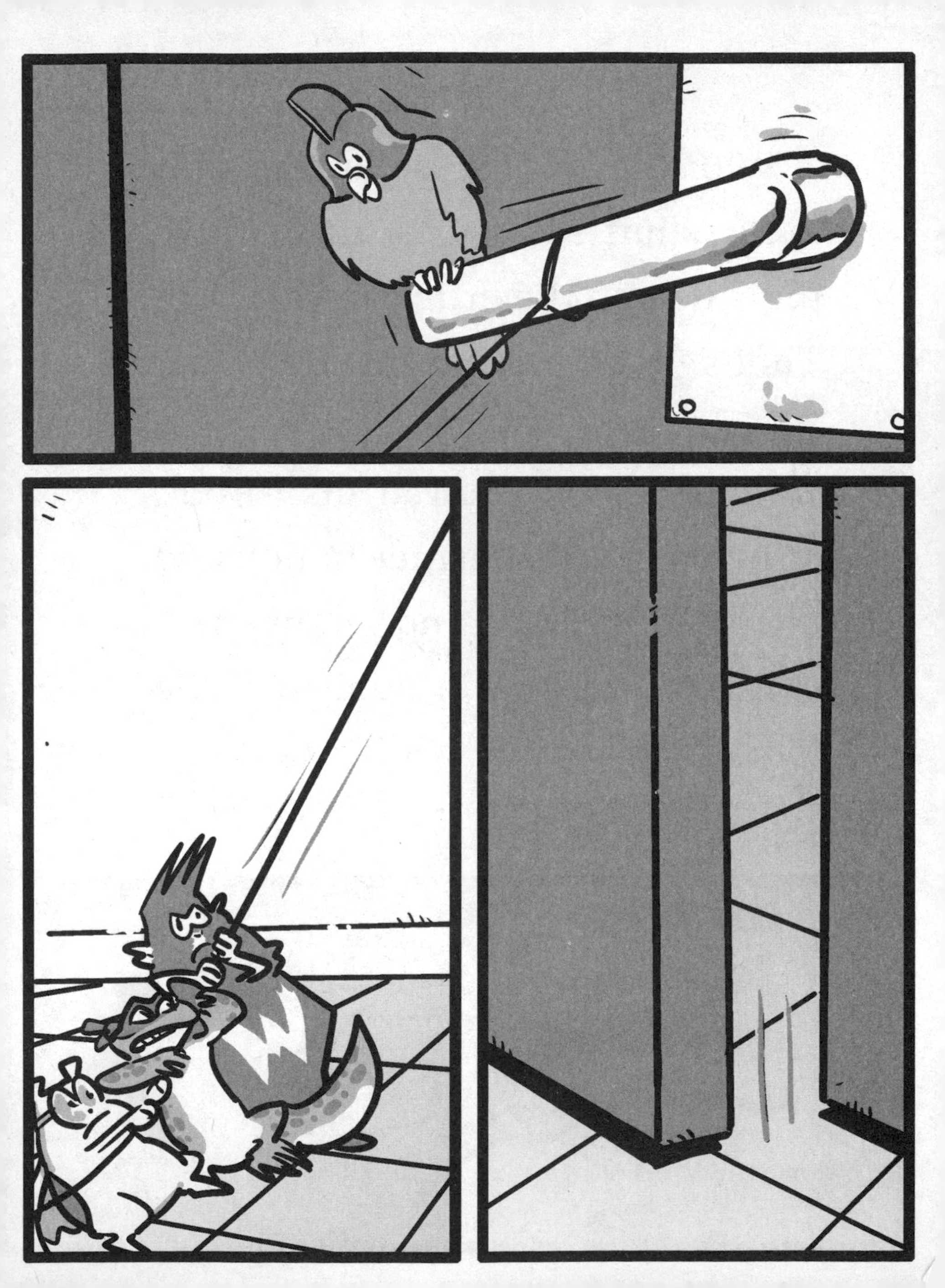

With the pantry open, the animals shuffled inside and made their way to the crack in the wall. That's where they'd first met Whiskerface.

Super Turbo cleared his throat. "Uh . . . Whiskerface?" he said uncertainly. Nothing happened. "Whiskerface?" he said a little louder this time. Still nothing. "WHISKERFACE!" he yelled.

WHO DARES DISTURB
MY BEAUTY REST?

I-I DON'T KNOW, SIR.

Well, that worked. Out crawled Whiskerface. And he did not look happy.

"What are you super*pests* doing here, disturbing my beauty rest—I mean . . . I mean . . . my evil naptime," Whiskerface fumbled.

Super Turbo proceeded to explain the situation to Whiskerface.

When he was done, Whiskerface twirled his long whiskers. "All right," he said. "I'll help you precious pampered pets. On one condition . . ."

6
FIRE!

“What’s your one condition?” Super Turbo asked. He braced himself for the worst. After all, Whiskerface had very recently tried to take over the whole school.

“I demand . . . ,” Whiskerface began.

The superpets waited with baited breath.

"I demand that you get me those chocolate cookies way up on the top shelf!" cried Whiskerface, pointing to a package of cookies. "I've been craving some chocolate and I—I can't reach them."

Super Turbo stifled his laughter. "That shouldn't be a problem," he assured Whiskerface. And with that, the Green Winger flew to the shelf and knocked the bag onto the floor. Cookies scattered everywhere, and Whiskerface stuffed his whiskered face. When he was finally full, he looked up and swallowed his last mouthful of cookie.

"To the science lab!" Whiskerface yelled.

LAB

Once in the science lab, Super Turbo pointed to the top of the desk, where the terrarium still sat. "Our enemy is up there," he said.

But Boss Bunny was sniffing the air with his bunny nose. "Do you smell what I smell?" he asked the superpets.

"Fine, you got me," admitted Whiskerface. "I had taco scraps

from the garbage for lunch."

Boss Bunny shook his head. "No, it's not that."

The other animals sniffed the air—though some of them had a *much* better sense of smell than others.

"It smells like something's burning," Super Turbo said suddenly.

"That's because something *is* burning!" cried the Green Winger.

A pile of papers on top of Dr. Garfield's desk was on fire!

"Quick . . . follow . . . me . . . ," said Warren not-so-quickly.

The superpets raced to the sink. Whiskerface, meanwhile, was starting to back out the door.

"Where do you think you're going?" yelled Super Turbo. "You're here to help us, aren't you?"

"I—uh—I think better about evil plans when I'm in my evil lair," Whiskerface said. But he soon realized he had nowhere to go. The door was locked and he certainly didn't have Boss Bunny's utility belt of supplies to help him get out.

The Superpets raced over to where the fire was and tipped the beaker of water toward the flames.

Super Turbo looked over toward the terrarium that housed the fire-breathing dragon. But the dragon wasn't in there. "It's on the loose!" cried Super Turbo.

7

THE LONGEST DAY EVER

The next morning, Turbo could barely open his eyes. Yesterday had been exhausting, and his cedar chips felt extra cozy today.

The night before, the superpets had searched for the fire-breathing dragon, but the dragon was nowhere to be found.

Whiskerface hadn't been much help, either. As he and his Rat Pack had headed back to the cafeteria, Whiskerface had promised the super-pets that he'd come up with a plan. So the pets were going to meet him after school was done for the day.

Meanwhile, in the science lab, Warren was still sound asleep.

WELL, CLASS, I HAD HOPED TO BE ABLE TO SHOW YOU HOW WE CAN BURN A CANDLE IN WATER.

I HAD STARTED TO PRACTICE THE EXPERIMENT LAST NIGHT, BUT I STEPPED AWAY FROM THE CLASSROOM FOR JUST A MOMENT AND WHEN I RETURNED,

ALL OF MY MATERIALS WERE RUINED. IT SEEMS THERE WAS A LEAK FROM THE CEILING, BECAUSE EVERYTHING WAS SOAKED! WE'LL HAVE TO POSTPONE THIS ONE.

When Warren woke up, he was glad to see that his kids were enjoying science class. Dr. Garfield always made it fun for them. But Warren knew it was really thanks to the superpets that the kids could even be here right now. If the pets hadn't put out that fire the dragon had started, there might not be a science lab anymore!

For all the superpets, the day dragged on . . .

AND ON . . .

AND ON . . .

AND ON . . .

AND ON . . .

AND ON . . .

AND ON . . .

Finally, the bell rang and the school emptied out. It was time to hear what Whiskerface had to say about getting rid of this evil fire-breathing dragon once and for all!

8

NEVER TRUST A RAT

In the cafeteria, Whiskerface was waiting for the superpets. Super Turbo was actually a little surprised that the rat had kept his word. His Rat Pack was gathered around him.

WELCOME, PAMPERED PETS. I'VE COME UP WITH MY MOST EVIL—I MEAN MY BEST—PLAN YET.

REMEMBER, WHISKERFACE, WE TOLD YOU WE DO NOT WANT ANY HARM DONE TO THE FIRE-BREATHING DRAGON.

Whiskerface proceeded to tell the Superpets his plan.

DOOR
STEP 1: YOU OPEN THE SCIENCE LAB DOOR FOR ME.
ME

ME, AGAIN
STEP 2: MY RAT PACK FORMS A PYRAMID. I'LL BE ON THE TOP, OF COURSE.

STEP 3: YOU PAMPERED PETS REMOVE THE LID OF THE TERRARIUM.

STEP 4: I USE THIS FEATHER TO TICKLE THE FIRE-BREATHING DRAGON.

WHILE IT'S IN THE
MIDDLE OF A LAUGHING
FIT, WE TIE IT UP.

STEP 5: WE LIFT THE
DRAGON OUT OF THE
TERRARIUM AND TOSS
IT THROUGH THE OPEN
WINDOW.

SuperTurbo had to admit: It didn't sound like a terrible plan. And there were some bushes right outside the science lab, so it's not like they'd hurt the dragon when they threw it out.

"To the science lab!" cried Super Turbo. And with that, he led his friends and the massive group of rats out of the cafeteria and down the hall.

When they reached the science lab, the pets opened the door. As promised, the Rat Pack formed a pyramid with Whiskerface on top. So the superpets kept their promise and worked together to lift off the top of the terrarium.

But what happened next was definitely *not* in the plan Whisker-face had laid out.

HA-HA-HA! YOU FELL FOR IT!

NOW THAT YOU'VE SET THE FIRE-BREATHING DRAGON FREE, I'M GOING TO FORCE IT TO HELP ME TAKE OVER THE SCHOOL. AND THEN...

Suddenly, something stirred inside the terrarium. The dragon had been sitting right in front of them, but it had blended in with the surrounding leaves. As it spoke, it almost looked like it was changing colors.

The fire-breathing dragon began to rise out of the terrarium. The superpets backed away. So did Whiskerface.

But the problem with backing away when you're part of a pyramid is . . . there's nowhere to go but down. The pyramid of rats toppled to the floor and Whiskerface ran from the lab, screaming.

With Whiskerface gone, the fire-breathing dragon turned on the Superpets.

9
A KA-WHAT?

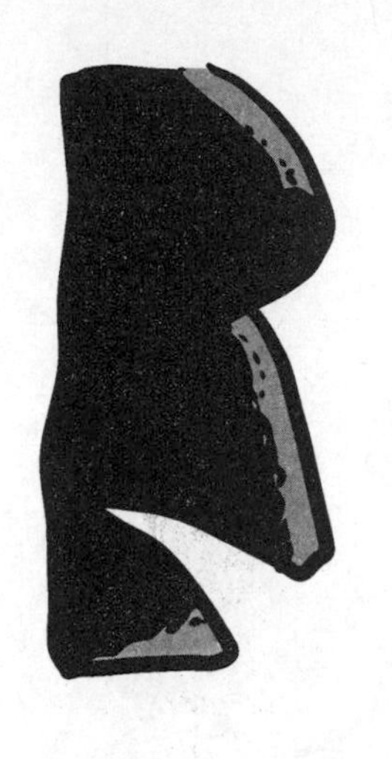

The dragon took a breath. Super Turbo was sure they were about to be extinguished.

But then something strange happened. Was the dragon . . . crying?

"Are you—are you okay?" asked Fantastic Fish, who clearly saw what Super Turbo saw.

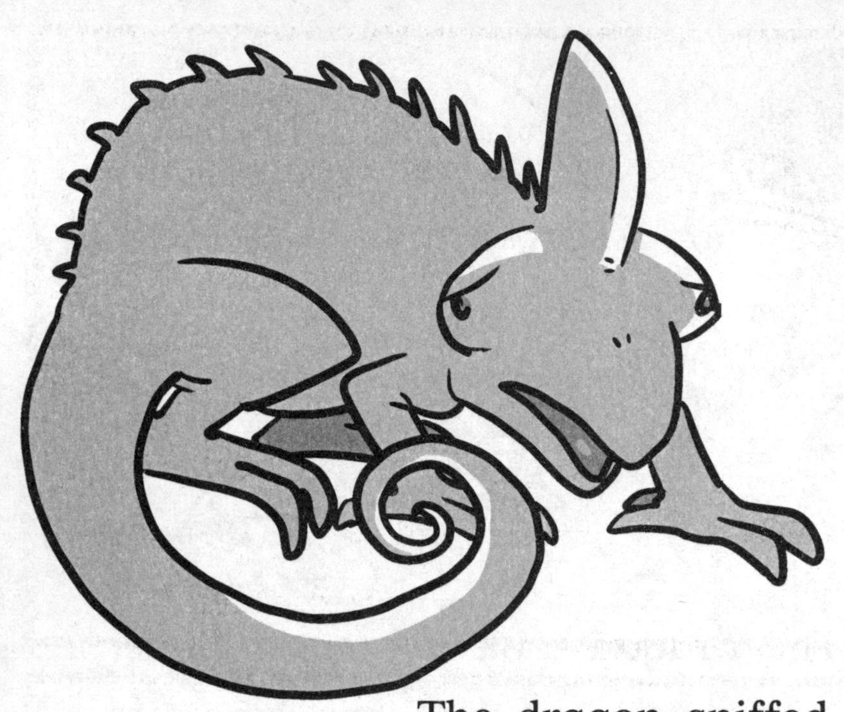

The dragon sniffed.

"Yeah, I guess. I know you guys want to get rid of me. I'm not sure why. I've been trying just to mind my own business. But it seems like I should go." The dragon turned to walk away.

WAIT! THE ONLY REASON WE WANTED TO GET RID OF YOU WAS SO THAT YOU DIDN'T SET FIRE TO THE SCHOOL!

SET FIRE TO THE SCHOOL?

THE SCIENCE TEACHER PRACTICALLY DID THAT THE OTHER NIGHT, BUT LUCKILY YOU GUYS WERE HERE TO PUT OUT THAT FLAME.
WHY WOULD I WANT TO DO ANYTHING TO HARM SUNNYVIEW ELEMENTARY?

I LOVE IT HERE!

BUT-
BUT AREN'T YOU A FIRE-BREATHING DRAGON?

At that, the dragon laughed. "A fire-breathing dragon? My name's Penelope, and I'm a chameleon."

"A ka-what?" asked Boss Bunny.

"A chameleon!" said Penelope. "I'm a special kind of lizard. I can change color, but I *certainly* cannot breathe fire," she explained.

The Superpets all let out one big sigh of relief.

"We're so sorry," said Super Turbo. "We were just trying to protect our school."

"That's okay. I'm just glad you don't actually want to get rid of me!" Penelope said happily.

"You . . . can . . . change . . . color?" Professor Turtle said slowly. "That . . .

explains . . . why we . . . couldn't . . . find . . . you."

Penelope explained that chameleons can change color to help them camouflage, or according to the temperature around them, or just depending on their mood! She showed them how she could be purple. Then pink. Then turquoise, yellow, orange, red, and back to green!

The Green Winger let out a whistle. "That is so cool," she said admiringly.

"So who was that weird little mouse who came in here

with you guys?" Penelope asked.

"He claims he's a rat," said Super Turbo. "And he sure acts like one. His name is Whiskerface and he's the real evil we have to protect the school from."

All the superpets nodded in agreement.

"Well, I'm no superpet, but if you ever need to give Whisker-face a good scare, I'll be here," said Penelope with a smile.

The superpets thanked her. It had been another long day, and it was time to get back to their classrooms.

The school had been saved yet again, thanks to . . .

THE SUPERPET SUPERHERO LEAGUE!

AND PENELOPE!

HERE'S A SNEAK PEEK AT SUPER TURBO'S NEXT ADVENTURE!

Super Turbo peered through his goggles.

He ran left, right, up, down, left again—*Wham!*

Super Turbo felt like he had run into a big furry brick wall.

"Whoa, are you okay?"

Turbo looked up to see his friend Angelina standing above him. She reached out a paw to help him back to his feet.

Like Turbo, Angelina was an official classroom pet—but of

Classroom A, instead of C. It had only been a little while ago that Turbo even learned that Angelina existed, but he liked her a lot. They had so much in common! They were both fuzzy, both ate food pellets, and both had pink ears and noses.

Of course, as a guinea pig, she was quite a bit bigger than Super Turbo, and was therefore a lot stronger too. She used her super strength, as well as her uncanny sense of direction, to fight evil as . . . the wondrous Wonder Pig!

"Thanks for coming over and

helping me train in this maze," said Super Turbo to Wonder Pig. "I think I almost found my way out."

Wonder Pig let out a laugh. "You've been running around in circles for the last five minutes!"

"I have?" asked Super Turbo.

"Yeah, follow me," said Wonder Pig.

A minute later Super Turbo and Wonder Pig were sitting outside the maze she had created out of books in the reading nook of Classroom C.

"I don't know how you do it," said Super Turbo, looking back. "You always know just which way to turn!"

"It's a gift," said Wonder Pig, "but every member of the Superpet Super League brings something special to the table."

"I guess that's true," said Super Turbo, thoughtfully.

"Yeah, and now you should use your special ability to go get us some food pellets!" said Wonder Pig, smiling. "All that maze-running has made me hungry."

Super Turbo sprang into action and "flew" to his cage where his food

was kept. A couple of minutes later he and Wonder Pig were sitting back in the book nook, enjoying a snack.

"See, I'm good at directions, and you can fly," said Wonder Pig, while munching. "Boy, I'd sure love to try flying . . . if only I had a cape. . . ."

CPSIA information can be obtained at www.ICGtesting.com
Printed in the USA
LVOW12s1238080514

384837LV00013B/179/P